To Sylvie's staff, particularly Alex—thank you!

SIMON & SCHUSTER
First published in Great Britain in 2017 by Simon & Schuster UK Ltd
1st Floor, 222 Gray's Inn Road, London, WC1X 8HB
A CBS Company

Published in the USA in 2016 by Beach Lane Books,
an imprint of Simon & Schuster Children's Publishing Division, New York

Copyright © 2016 by Marla Frazee.

A CIP catalogue record for this book is available from the British Library upon request

ISBN: 978-1-4711-6110-0 (PB)
ISBN: 978-1-4711-6111-7 (ebook)

Printed in China

10 9 8 7 6 5 4 3 2 1

www.simonandschuster.co.uk

introducing

the

Bossier BABY

AS HERSELF!

by Marla Frazee

SIMON & SCHUSTER
London New York Sydney Toronto New Delhi

From the moment his baby sister arrived,

the Boss Baby had a feeling
that change was in the air.

The first thing the new executive did was outline her business plan and restructure the organisation . . .

from the top

down.

Then she demoted the Boss Baby and promoted herself to Chief Executive Officer, CEO for short.

The CEO was bossier than
the Boss Baby had ever been.

Which seems impossible.

Even so, the staff were strangely delighted.
The Boss Baby had never seen them so happy.

This made him miserable.

So did her perks.

There was the organic catering service.

Aromatherapy.

Stress management.

Afternoon spinning.

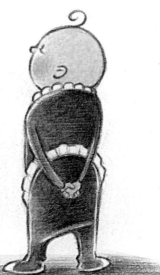

A full-time
social
media
team.

And, of course, the private limo.

The Boss Baby had
had some perks
in his time, but
nothing like this.

He was furious.

But the CEO and staff
paid no attention
to him.

No matter what he did.

Where he did it.

Or how outrageous it was.

Finally the Boss Baby just gave up.
He made no demands, had no fits,
exhibited no temper, and weirdly
had no opinions about anything at all.

This was highly irregular.

But the CEO knew what to do.

She wasn't CEO for nothing!

And at last the company was back to business,
operating productively, cooperatively, and efficiently . . .

most of the time.